This Little Tiger book belongs to:

_____

_____

_____

With thanks to TJ, TJ, CJ and PJ – S U

LITTLE TIGER PRESS
1 The Coda Centre, 189 Munster Road,
London SW6 6AW
www.littletigerpress.com • First published in Great Britain 2011
This edition published 2012
Text and illustrations copyright © Sam Usher 2011
Sam Usher has asserted his right to be identified as the author and illustrator
of this work under the Copyright, Designs and Patents Act, 1988
A CIP catalogue record for this book is available from the British Library
All rights reserved • ISBN 978-1-84895-088-7 • Printed in China
LTP/1800/0544/1112 • 10 9 8 7 6 5 4 3 2

Sam Usher

Can You See SASSOON?

LITTLE TIGER PRESS

LONDON

This is **Sassoon.** He likes to hide.
Can you find him? Look inside!

Bobbing balloons are floating by,
Soaring slowly through the sky.

Can you see Sassoon there too,
Hiding away from me and you?

WHAT a picnic!
Ham with custard,
Cheese with icing,
jelly and mustard.

Sassoon is hiding. Can you see?
He's peeking out at you and me.

A pile of presents!
What's inside?
An elephant?
A water-slide?

Sssurprise!

I can't see him here, can you?
Perhaps Sassoon is
wrapped up too!

Sailing in the summer sun,
There's a boat for everyone!

WHAT a busy boating lake!
We'll never see that silly snake.

Golden Hound

Frilly knickers, fancy frocks,
Spotty dresses, stripy socks.

Giant pants flap in the air.
But where's Sassoon?
He MUST be there!

Spots and stripes
and peeping eyes.
There's toys of
every shape and size.

Oh dear!
I can't begin to guess
Where he can be
in all this mess!

Where is he now? In outer space!
He's joined a whizzy rocket-race.

Finish

I can see the stars and moon,
But where, oh where
are YOU, Sassoon?

So many books,
all full of fun!
I want to stay
and read each one.

Baking Cakes for busy snakes

Sassoon's a Balloon

The Snake Spotter's Guide

How to Wrap an Elephant

SLIDING AND HIDING

BALLOONING for Tigers

Snake Charming for Beginners

Ssspectacles

The Rubber Duck Mystery

Petty & Betty

Mat Sssea My life on the ocean waves

ABC

The Com SNAK

Sassoon! Come out!
Where have you gone?
This game has gone on
far too long!

ALL his friends are hiding now!
We have to find him here, but HOW?
Shhhh, everyone! Here's what we'll do:
Let's creep up quietly, ready –

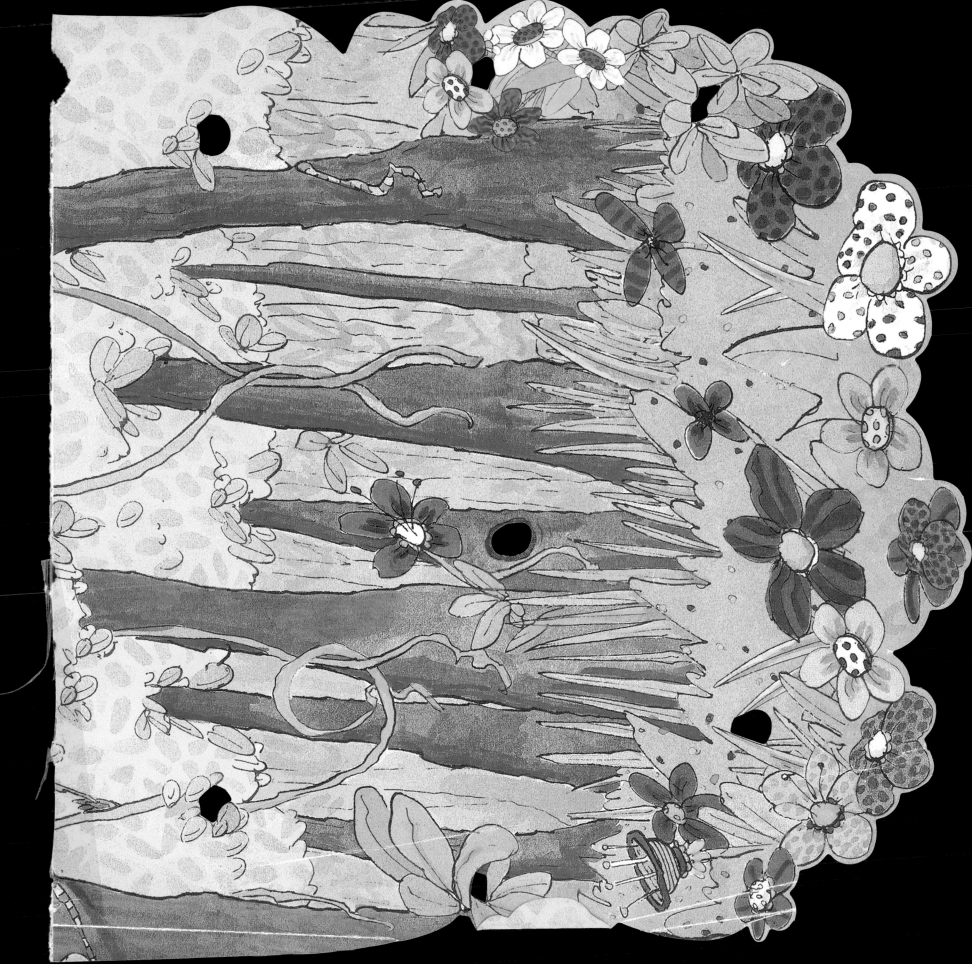

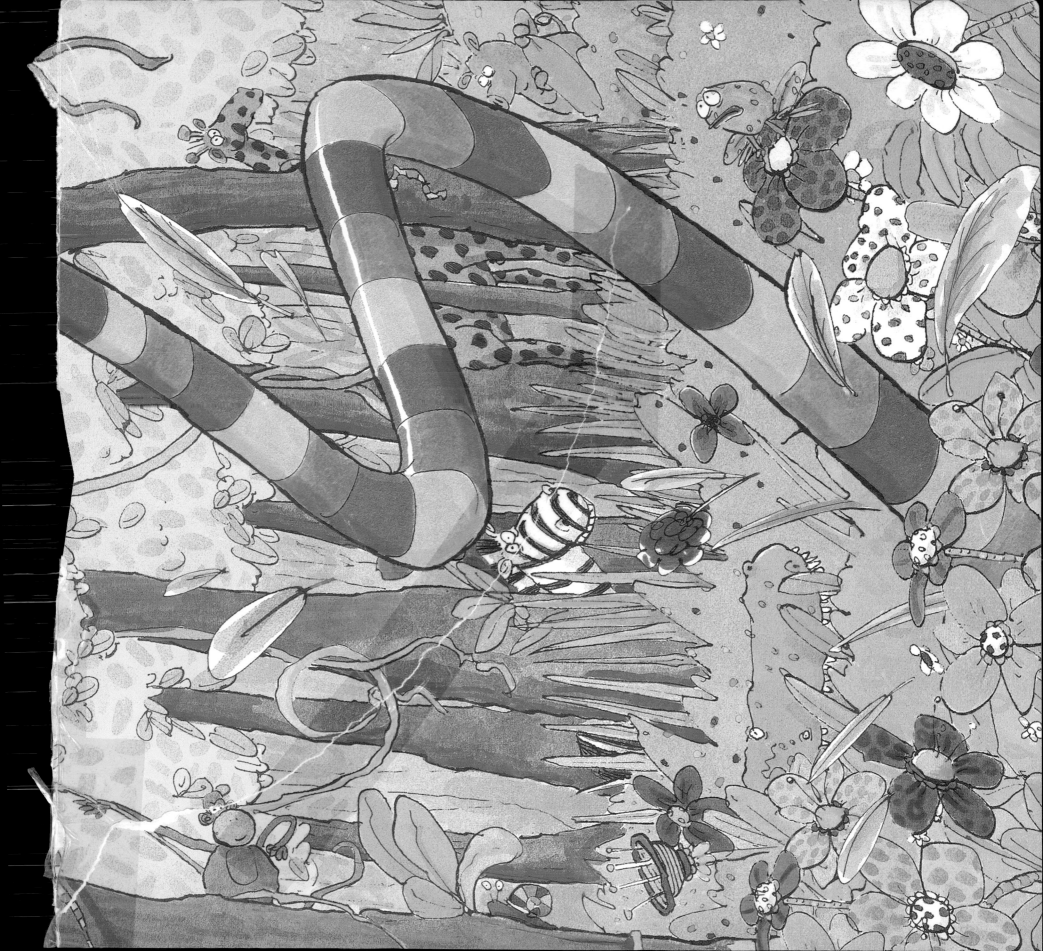

More Sssssuper books from Little Tiger Press!

Star Friends
Tracey Corderoy
Alison Edgson

Oh Dylan!
A soft-to-touch book
Tracey Corderoy · Tina Macnaughton

The Great Monster Hunt
Norbert Landa
Tim Warnes

Don't Wake the Bear, Hare!
Steve Smallman
Caroline Pedler

Sylvia and Bird
Catherine Rayner

Bright Stanley
Matt Buckingham

For information regarding any of the above titles
or for our catalogue, please contact us:
Little Tiger Press, 1 The Coda Centre,
189 Munster Road, London SW6 6AW
Tel: 020 7385 6333 • Fax: 020 7385 7333
E-mail: info@littletiger.co.uk • www.littletigerpress.com